Scott finds a kitten trapped deep in a
rubbish bin. Despite the council rules
about pets, Scott takes the kitten home
and persuades his mum to keep it.
Unfortunately Mrs Prescott from along
the balcony finds out about Scrap and
she and Scott have a bitter argument
about stolen milk. To prove his
innocence, Scott has to find out who is
the *real* thief. The answer comes as a
surprise.

*   *   *   *

Bernard Ashley, a headmaster of a
primary school in London, is very well-
known and highly respected as a
children's writer and has won many
prizes for his books.

*   *   *   *

"The story is good because Bernard
Ashley, as a London Head himself, really
knows his background." *Junior
Bookshelf*

"A shrewd eye on character, matched
and pointed up by some cleverly
individualised line drawings, give depth
to this short book." *Growing Point*

A BIT OF
GIVE AND TAKE

Bernard Ashley

Illustrated by Trevor Stubley

YOUNG CORGI BOOKS

A BIT OF GIVE AND TAKE
A YOUNG CORGI BOOK : 0 552 52348 8

PRINTING HISTORY
First published in Great Britain in 1984 by
Hamish Hamilton Children's Books
Young Corgi edition published 1986
Reprinted 1986, 1987, 1988, 1991, 1994, 1996 (twice), 1997

Young Corgi Books are published by Transworld Publishers Ltd,
61–63 Uxbridge Road, Ealing, London W5 5SA,
in Australia by Transworld Publishers (Australia) Pty Ltd,
15–25 Helles Avenue, Moorebank, NSW 2170,
and in New Zealand by Transworld Publishers (NZ) Ltd,
3 William Pickering Drive, Albany, Auckland.

Printed and bound in Great Britain by
Cox & Wyman Ltd, Reading, Berkshire.

A BIT OF
GIVE AND TAKE

Chapter 1

SCOTT HAD NEVER been a great one for hearing things. His world was filled too much with noise — with traffic and aircraft and radios, and with his own hectic life. Ms Peters in school was always on about him not listening. His sister Sandra kept saying his ears were only there to use up a bit of extra skin. And his mother, to get an answer from him, usually had to shout till she made an eye water.

But that night after school he was the only one who heard the noise. All the others charged at top speed past the big

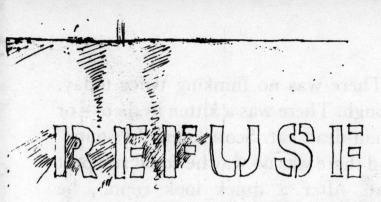

REFUSE

refuse bin beneath the flats. But Scott heard the sound coming from inside it – and Scott was the one who stopped.

It was faint and hopeless, a weak, broken note like a whisper for help.

Scott let the others go and looked up. The bin was tall and broad and fed by a chute from the tower block above. It was a dangerous thing to be in. A few seconds of clatter was all you heard before an avalanche of bottles and cans and old food came bursting down, sharp and hard, from above. If someone threw your ball in there you thought twice before you climbed in to get it back.

There was no thinking twice today, though. There was a kitten in there – or a half-dead cat. Scott knew the sound. And there was no way he could run past that. After a quick look round, he backed a few paces, put on a sudden spurt like someone at the high jump, and ran hard for the bin. When he got within reach, he leapt. His hands clawed at the top, his feet scrabbled at the smooth, broad side. And with a trembling pull on his arms he heaved himself up to the top.

Balanced there, he stopped. Scott hadn't thought about it while he was getting up, but it could be scary, not knowing what disaster you were going to see. He hoped it wouldn't be something really horrible. Like a just-alive cat. Or a cat with something broken. He wouldn't know what to do about

anything like that. As if he were looking at a nasty scene on the television, he narrowed his eyes into slits and took a quick look down at the uneven waste of rubbish.

At first he couldn't make anything out. As hard and as fast as he looked he couldn't see any sign of life. But he could hear the sound again, louder now in the metal ring of the bin. He was jumpy about staying where he was for too long. The others would come back looking for him. Or the caretaker would have him. So, quickly, Scott made up his mind. He'd have to get right in.

Carefully, he lifted a leg over the battered rim and let himself down. His knees and toecaps rubbed the ashy side as his arms strained out at full stretch. It was a long way down. The rubbish was lower than it had looked from the

top. It gave as he tried to stand on it.
And looking up, the chute was darker
and more dangerous from down there.
Any second now – and who knew what
could come tipping on top of him?

But before he could think too hard about it, Scott heard the noise again. A bit longer, a bit stronger. It was some helpless thing and from the sound of it, it could tell that someone was near. Someone who might help it. It wasn't until he put his foot on something – just his foot, not all his weight – that the creature cried out sharply in sudden pain, and Scott could tell where the sound was coming from.

Chapter 2

THE OTHER KIDS came back, running
past the bin and shouting out Scott's
name. One of their hands smacked the
metal near his head. But he kept very
still. He crouched, dead quiet, in that
terrible smell. And all the time he
stroked the matted fur of the trapped
kitten and hoped to heaven it wouldn't
miaouw. Because this was going to be
his secret. There were some things you
wanted to share straight away; but
there were other things you wanted to
keep till you were ready. And this was
one of them – an animal which needed

help. Something which needed him.

When the sounds of the others died away, Scott started shifting around. Keeping his weight well away from the kitten, he began to use his hands like a surgeon. He thanked God he wasn't all shaky like the old man who lived on his balcony. Or all impatient like moany Mrs Prescott. Carefully, he lifted away little bits of stuff which he tried not to think about. Bits of dirty cotton wool, hair-brush hairs, slippery food: scattered all over with sticky tea-leaves like wet brown confetti. He wriggled aside a gaping tin and he heaved at a bursting wet newspaper parcel. Till at last, when he was starting to think he couldn't crouch like that any more, the last thing gave, and the kitten was free.

"There y'are!" he said. "Got you. How about that, boy?"

But if he'd thought the freed kitten was going to jump into his arms for a thank-you nuzzle he was wrong. The little thing – all weak, thorny claws and stylus teeth – stared at Scott with hate and spat at him with fear.

Scott was up to that, though. He'd always been as ready for a clout as for a kiss.

"I never done it," he said. "I never tipped you in here. I'm your mate. See . . . ?

He stayed there while the light began to fade. He stopped thinking about the chute above. A finger here, a hand there, he touched at the kitten with care. And he talked all the time — soothing, loving nonsense. At last, after half an hour, he knew it was time to stop. Either he'd done it, or he hadn't. Either the kitten would run, or it would stay. Without a bottle of milk in his pocket there wasn't much he could do about it. But he made a few final promises. In case it had learned the word milk he used it over and over, told it about the milk, milk, milk it would have to drink when it got to his flat. He went silly about the word, because he really wanted the kitten to stick with him — even if he did sound daft talking to it. I could really do with a kitten to call my own, Scott thought.

He pulled himself back to the top of the bin with the kitten in his coat. Shifting his weight again, he held it in his hand like a horse in a sling. And, reaching as far down the outside as he could, Scott dangled: till just when he was in danger of falling down himself, he let the kitten go.

Drop!

With all the instinct of a full-grown cat, the kitten fell on all fours. Scott looked at it from upside down. It was funny the way cats knew how to be grown up so quick, he thought – and then stayed running and jumping till they died. Different to humans. Yes, it would definitely be good to have a cat, he decided.

As quietly as he could, Scott followed it down to the ground. He sniffed at himself, hoped he wasn't too smelly.

Still, he thought, what if I am? It was worth it to save the life of a kitten. Even if it was tottering away from him.

"Milk. Milk!" He tried the word again. The kitten stopped at the sound, and stared. And, to Scott's great surprise, it suddenly opened its mouth in a big miaouw and started to come back towards him.

Chapter 3

HE MADE UP HIS MIND he wouldn't scare
it by going up in the lift. The thing had
had enough of dark, smelly places for
one day, hadn't it? So with its fragile
head under the stroke of his fingers, and
its trembling body tucked inside his
coat, he climbed the stairs to his balcony. There were ninety-one of them.
When the lifts weren't working that
made seven lots of unlucky thirteen he
reckoned – even for tough people like
him.

Lifts or stairs, though, there was no
bad luck tonight, he thought. Just the

opposite. Tonight was a great night, because tonight he'd got a kitten, and the kitten had got him. And he was sure his mum would let him keep it, in the end. Now she was on her own she was easy, if he kept on about something long enough.

The balcony was stained where the rain rarely got. The ledges were dusty, and squashed dog-ends skidded about. Outside the front doors plastic holders or tiles or just grey rings told where the milk bottles went.

Scott took great care not to kick an empty. Kicking empties brought out the old people quicker than the postman's footsteps.

"Look!" Scott spoke firmly to the puppet-like bundle in his coat. "See where you live? High, i'n it?" Carefully, he let the kitten look out, well back from

the parapet. "You can't jump down there, boy. Hope you're gonna like it."

Scott and Sandra and their mother hadn't left their old house all that long. And they wouldn't be here for ever, it was only for the time being. Scott still had very mixed feelings about the flats. Being all this high up and having the lifts was still a bit of a novelty. But being so close to all the old people on the balcony was definitely a drawback. You couldn't do anything without upsetting one or other of them.

And tonight was no different. Nothing was private. The door behind him opened quietly – and he jumped at the sudden sound of a loud voice.

"Who's that hanging about? What you up to?" It was Mrs Prescott, as fierce in her doorway as a roused Alsatian. "What you lurking about here for?

I don't like people lurking about outside here."

"It's only me. Scott."

But that didn't seem to give her any joy.

"You need telling a lot, don't you? Here, what you got there?"

She could switch her attack like Liverpool.

"Nothing!"

"Yes, you have, down your coat. I know you kids." She made it sound as if all kids went round with secret things down their coats.

Scott tried to push the kitten out of sight. He didn't know why, but he knew it was best kept a secret from Mrs Prescott. But the sudden movement scared the kitten again. It wasn't ready to trust anyone yet. Its frightened miaouw was loud and throaty.

"It's a cat! You've got a blessed cat down there!"

"It's not! It's a kitten. I just saved it."

"Kittens *are* cats. Flea-ridden things!" Mrs Prescott scratched herself as she said it. "And what's more . . ." She took in a deep breath to make some other remark. But Scott didn't stay to listen. He held his kitten tight with one hand and pushed into his flat with the other.

Stupid old woman! he thought. Why couldn't people like her mind their own business?

Chapter 4

"WHAT THE DEVIL have you got there?"

Scott's mother bumped into him. She came out of her bedroom behind a dull rainbow of washing and almost smothered the kitten in it.

"What's *that*? Is it alive?"

Sandra screamed. She loved something to scream at. She screamed the way normal people just gave you a look.

"'Course it's alive. I saved it. It's a kitten."

Mrs Turner threw the washing on the floor, there in the hallway.

"A kitten? You don't reckon you're

keeping that, do you?"

"He's not keeping that, Mum!"

"I *am*! I saved it from death!" Scott shouted it at them. In all their ups and downs he'd found out that if you were as loud as they were – if you sounded as *definite* – you stood a good chance of getting your own way. "He'll die without me!"

"Good job!" Sandra slammed her bedroom door. "I don't want it crawling on my bed!"

Mrs Turner stood there with a hand on her hip and the other on her forehead. "I can't feed that!" she said. "I'm hard enough pushed to feed you two. What do you want to do a stupid thing like this for? Take it back down, Scott. Let it go, 'fore it starts getting ideas."

Scott cuddled it closer. "No! It won't be no trouble. It can eat what's leftover. Sandra never eats her dinner up."

"I'm not arguing the toss, boy. Do you know the price of a pint of milk? I can't *afford* another mouth to feed."

Scott could see his mother beginning to harden. He had the horrible feeling he was on the way to losing: he did lose sometimes.

So he cried. He dropped his lip and

started to grizzle. He forced two big tears – both out of the same eye – on to his cheek.

"Someone's already tried to kill him. He thinks he's safe now. He'll never trust no one no more."

Mrs Turner's shoulders drooped. "But what about the mess?"

"They do it in a box. I'll get a box and put some dirt in it. Honest, I won't let him be no trouble, Mum. Mum . . ."

Mrs Turner stared at Scott and Scott stared at her.

"Oh, you kids!"

The kitten, not knowing how its life had just been fought for, looked calmly out from Scott's coat. Its heart, still beating at five times the speed of quartz, was making less of a thump in its thin body now.

"Well, it's down to you, you hear me? I don't want no come-backs."

"O.K! Great!" And Scott would have cheered, except for scaring his kitten.

But who was his kitten? Scott hadn't thought about that. What was he going to call him?

Suddenly, it came. *Scrap*. Scott stroked its head again. Yes, Scrap. That seemed about right for a kitten saved from the rubbish bin.

Mrs Turner scooped at her washing.

Scott turned to start looking for a box. But before either of them had really made a move, Sandra came bursting out of the kitchen. She had something in her hand. It was the council rent book.

"See this?" she asked, with a false sad look on her face. "See what this says?"

"What's up with you?" Scott didn't pay the rent, did he?

"No cats!" said Sandra. "No pets except birds in cages and fishes in tanks. It's one of the council rules – see?"

Scott stared at the book she was waving in front of him.

"That's why you found him. People have to get shot of pets, or the council has them put to sleep."

Chapter 5

SCOTT DIDN'T SLEEP very well that night. He felt like a soldier trying to close his eyes in the middle of a battle. He'd won the home side of things – his mum would let Scrap stay. Now his enemy was the council and everyone else outside. He had to be ready to save Scrap at every moment. The only thought to cheer him up was that they weren't in that flat for ever. It was only a half-way place till a house came up – and pets were allowed in houses, he'd made Sandra check. So if he could hold out with Scrap till that happened, he'd be

all right, Scott thought.

And Scrap had settled well. He'd
eaten a fish finger and a squashed oven-
chip for his tea, drunk half a saucer of
milk, used his box, and gone to sleep
with Scott. But he twitched once or
twice on the pillow, and Scott started
wondering if cats and kittens could
dream. If so, was Scrap dreaming about
the bad things that had happened to
him? About the bad owner who'd
thrown him out? Or was he playing
some game in his sleep? Scott hoped
that was it.

Anyway, if Scrap stayed indoors and didn't get on people's nerves, the next day could be the start of a really good new life. For both of them. And with that thought, Scott at last went off to sleep.

Some hopes! Scott had hardly got out of his front door next morning when the fresh attack began.

"Is it you, had the milk off my step?"

Mrs Prescott's door had opened so suddenly it made Scott jump. It made him look guilty already.

"No!" It was true, but he always said "no" first, anyway. It was safest, because they were all the same along the balcony – all these old people who waited for him, grabbed him any time they wanted, said he'd done things he hadn't.

"Well, someone's had it!" Mrs Pres-

cott had her arms folded and pressed, as if she was only just holding her hands back from hitting him. She frowned, and said it again slowly, as if it would scare him enough to get the truth out. "I tell you, someone's had it. The last two mornings!"

"Not me. I never have no milk, you can ask my mum." Scott pulled a face to show how much he never drank milk. "Erk! I wouldn't drink it if I was starving to death."

"No, but your cat would, wouldn't it?" Mrs Prescott's voice was filled with meaning, and her bony finger poked him where Scrap had been. "As if it wasn't against the rules having cats in these flats, you've got the blessed nerve to go stealing other people's milk for it! Well, I'm not letting this go past, Scott Turner, and you can tell your mum the same. I've been too soft by half with all you lot!"

She stared a hard look at him and slammed her door. Scott shrugged. That'd be the day – when he *wasn't* being got at for doing something wrong! Eating the last Jaffa-cake, missing his aim in the lavatory, rubbing out Sandra's favourites on the video: always something. Every day was a booby-trap for him. If he got through a day from one end to the other without an explosion he could reckon himself dead lucky.

But today really *did* mean trouble, with what Old Mother Prescott had just said. She meant business, Scott could tell that. What he'd feared – she'd got it in for Scrap now. It'd be no good telling her this was the first morning he'd had his kitten. She never

believed anyone. He'd just about got his mum on his side. But she wouldn't stand up to a lot of going-on from Mrs Prescott about stolen milk for pets.

And he wasn't even off the balcony yet! At the end of it was one of the trickiest bits of all – getting past old Mr Harding's door. That old man could hear a trainer on tip-toe, and he got Scott every time he wanted him whether he crept past like a burglar or tried to make a run for it.

And today was just the same. The old man was all ready to grab him. He came out like a jack-in-the-box and got hold of his collar.

"You, boy! I want a word with you!"

"Me? What for?" Had old Harding seen his cat as well?

Mr Harding's fingers dug in and rocked him, not so much with a shake

45

as with a giant tremble he couldn't stop. "I'll tell you what for. Just you keep your noisy larks for down the park, you hear me? I'm fed up with you kicking up a shindy out here till all hours. Have a bit of regard for your elders for a change. Some people get to bed early, you want to remember that."

"Get off! I'm not allowed down the park!" Scott shouted. He twisted himself free and ran off, rubbing his shoulder where the pinch had hurt. The silly old man! They shouldn't put kids on the same balcony as old blokes, even as a stop-gap! Still, at least the old man hadn't been on about Scrap.

The lifts weren't working again so he swung round seven corners and jumped down seven flights of stairs to get to the ground. He raced through the estate to school and got in just before bell-time.

For a while he even forgot about Mrs Prescott and her threat to his kitten. Things go from your mind a bit when you get out of breath.

Chapter 6

INSIDE, THE BUILDING had a special smell
all of its own. There was never a whiff of
it anywhere else on the estate. It smelt
of *school*, and it always made Scott feel
heavy inside. It slowed him down, like
wearing his winter coat. He knew
exactly what it was. It was a mixture of
the red dirt they threw over the floor
and swept all up again (which showed
how barmy the caretaker was) and the
smell of empty milk crates by the
kitchen.

And smelling the milk as he went in
that morning brought things back

straight away, pulled him down again. Stupid Old Mother Prescott! As if he'd be rotten enough to have the milk off her step! It'd be a laugh, he thought, if it wasn't for the fact that they weren't allowed cats in their flats. And that Mrs Prescott was just the rotten sort to go marching down the Town Hall to complain . . .

He sat at the table and stared at a

maths card. He pulled a face at it. He'd got a problem to work out much harder than this old rubbish, he thought. Get this stuff right and you got a tick. Get it wrong and you got a cross. So what? But get the Old Mother Prescott thing wrong and he was going to lose Scrap – and that was *really* something to worry about.

The card went into a blur in front of his eyes. The noise around him seemed to fade as he tried to puzzle out his problem.

What if he pretended he *had* taken the milk, and he said he was sorry? Would that get him off? He screwed up his face. No, not much of a chance, he thought. He'd said "sorry" to Old Mother Prescott before, and all she did was go on worse than when she'd started.

He looked round the room, tried to wink at a couple of mates, but his eye didn't want to do it. He'd never sat down and wanted to get something sorted out so badly.

He saw the gerbil asleep in his cage. Lucky thing! Not a worry in the world. Pity *he* hadn't been born a gerbil, he thought. Nothing to do but eat and sleep and play. And suddenly his eyes came sharp. For a wild minute he thought he'd done it, really got the answer. What if – yes, what if he put up his hand for taking the gerbil home?

And when he got upstairs he put it through Old Mother Prescott's letter-box? All he'd have to do was wait outside till she screamed, then rush in with Scrap to save her. Scrap would be brilliant with a titchy little thing that went fast. She'd be dead pleased there was a cat living next door then!

But Scott soon came down to earth. The gerbil wouldn't be dead pleased, would he? He'd just be dead! And that would be as bad as Scrap being put to sleep. So that wasn't so brilliant after all. Under his breath Scott said a few things. He banged his head with his hand to try to knock out a good idea.

"Nice to see Scott quiet and really thinking," Ms Peters said. "A lesson for all of us. Good boy." Everyone looked. Scott switched smiles on and off for them. He turned his back and threw

some answers down on to the paper. He even had a feeling some of them were right. But that couldn't cheer him up any more. Nothing that didn't work out his real-life worry ever would, he thought.

Chapter 7

THE ANSWER CAME from an odd direction, like scoring a goal from a bounce off the roof. Without warning, instead of P.E. they all went into the hall for a talk by a man called One of our Special Guests. And by the time he'd finished Scott thought he really was special, he'd have him back any day. He was really good for a change, the sort you could take plenty of. He was young, and funny, and what Scott liked best was the way he got kids out to help him and had everyone falling about while they played silly games. He made them try

to do things with one hand held behind their backs, and he gave them tricks to do with their legs tied together. They had to try to catch pretend buses, and go up and down the drama blocks. It was really good. One kid was a great laugh: Wayne, in the fourth year. He ran up and down the blocks like a cat. Till the man tied a stick up his leg. Wayne was all sure of himself, thought he could do it again, wasn't going to be beaten. But he got all bent over and couldn't swing his leg up at all. The look of surprise on his face was something you wished you had a camera for. Of course, the serious bit had to come at the end, it always did, but this time it had Scott even higher up on his knees with excitement.

"Think of the old people near you," the man said. "We can't just untie their

hands and legs and make their limbs work, not if they're bad. Once upon a time these people were boys and girls like you. But now they can never run for buses, never get to the ground floor if the lifts go wrong. And as for earning a few extra pennies if they're hard up, well, that's impossible, so they often just go without . . ."

Scott listened with his mouth open. Because the man was talking about the people along his balcony. Mr Harding, Old Mother Prescott. Was this why they were always so ratty? Perhaps they hated not dodging about any more. Perhaps they were jealous of not growing old like animals did, like Scrap would, still able to do things. And already Scott's head had begun to go swimmy with the beauty of a plan that had suddenly come to him.

Meanwhile, the man went on. "Now, here's what you do. You get your parents' permission and you go and do something to help an old person *you* know. Talk to them. Let them know you care. Take them a present – it doesn't have to be harvest-time to do that. And it doesn't have to be anything special, either – a cake, a packet of tea, they'll be delighted with that. It'll mean the world to them. And for every child who does something, there's a special present – a ball . . ."

A ball! Scott stared at it. And what a ball, too! It got him up even higher, made Ms Peters tell him to sit down on his bottom again.

It was small and shiny with a bounce like a ball on the moon.

"Every time you play with this special ball – jumping to catch it and

running after it – I want you to think of all the old people who can never do these things any more."

It was a ball to beat all other balls. Definitely a ball to have. Wouldn't Scrap enjoy playing games with that? Scott thought. Something else good on top of keeping him.

Because Scott knew what he would do. That was easy. He'd take Old Mother Prescott a bottle of milk from outside the kitchen. He'd go without custard on his school dinners so he wasn't really stealing it, but he'd get one from the crate and give it to her – to make up for what that thief had taken off her step. Then, when she saw what a kind kid he was, she wouldn't go and tell on his cat, would she?

It wasn't hard to do, either, when the time came. The cooks were always too

busy moaning to take any notice, so no
one heard the crate go as he lifted out
one of the full bottles. It went under his
coat to the cloakroom. And there it
stood as good as gold till it was time to
take it home and use it – for an Old
Folk, for a ball, and for something to
help keep hold of his kitten.

65

Chapter 8

SCOTT GOT BACK to the flats quicker than
if he had been being chased. He raced
up the stairs two at a time with the milk
bottle in one hand and his *Help the Old
Folk* form in the other. He was filled
with a bursting feeling of doing good.
As he rattled at the letter-box of Mrs
Prescott's flat his chest was pressed out
hard with all the kindness inside him.

Whoosh! She had to *live* behind that
door, he thought, the way she opened it
so fast.

"Got you!" she said. "You knocking-
down-Ginger now?"

66

"No! 'Course not! I got you this." He held out the milk bottle, which was running on the outside with little rivulets of hand grime. He wiped them and smiled at her like a hero.

"And what's that for?"

"For you – to drink, 'cos yours got took."

"Eh?" Mrs Prescott looked at him hard, and tipped her head on one side to see if he could be trusted. "Who've you been robbing to pay me back?"

"No one. It's from the school. Like harvest. It's a present . . ."

She put the milk inside her door and looked out at the weather. "But it's nowhere near harvest . . ." Her head was back straight again, and she was frowning.

"It's special, see. You have to sign this." With a big flap he brought the paper out from behind his back. He smiled again and waited to see her read the words and go all happy round the face. Already he could feel Scrap thanking him.

She was a quick reader. It took her about three seconds.

"*Help the Old Folk!*" she shouted.

68

"Help the – *what?!*" She grabbed the door post to stop herself going over. "Is this your idea of a . . . a . . . ?" She couldn't get it out. She'd run out of breath, just like the man had said old people did. She took a great gulp, pulled herself up. "I may not see thirty again!" she croaked. "Or even . . . forty . . . but I am not an Old Folk by a very, very, *very* long chalk!" Her breath was coming back, and now it was Scott doing the frowning. "First you take my milk, and now you take the mickey! You horrible little . . ." And then words failed her again. She suddenly slammed the door, and the whole block shook with it. And Scott could only stare as his screwed-up piece of paper fell where she'd thrown it. Dropping like his spirits down seven storeys to the street.

He knotted together a long string of

rude words. What a rotten turn-out! After all his trying hard, another day had gone off in his face. And there'd be no super-ball tomorrow; but what was a million times worse, what he'd done to try to help had made it all the more definite now that Scrap would get taken away, and put to sleep by the council.

Chapter 9

IT CAME TO Scott in bed, lying there with Scrap snuggled up on his chest. While the wall went in and out like an eardrum to the sound of Sandra's stereo, another answer – the only answer now – started to dance in front of him. Of course, it was clear as day when he thought about it. Why hadn't it come to him before? The real thief just had to be found. Then Old Mother Prescott would *know* he hadn't stolen her milk for Scrap. She'd know Scrap wasn't going to be a trouble along the balcony. No, that was it, and there was no way round it. It was down to Scott to find out. Was it the milkman doing a fiddle? The paper-girl getting thirsty? One of the kids being clever? Well, there was only one way to see. Scott had to be out on that balcony early next morning to catch the person in the act.

Easier said than done, of course: Scott knew that. Getting up early was something no one was good at in his flat. He did get off to sleep at last – a long time after Scrap – but he kept dreaming about not waking up in time, and his sleep was as thin as the sheets.

Which meant that when it was almost time to do the getting up he slid steeply off into a really warm, deep slumber. But the *Capital* voice on his clock radio went on and on till it got through to him at last, and he climbed out of bed in his top clothes and tiptoed across to the door of the flat.

Scrap – who all this was for – did his best to ruin everything. He wound round Scott's legs to love him and trip him. He miaouwed loud enough to wake the flat. And when Scott put his hand over his mouth to keep him quiet, he gave him a nip.

And then the door-chain. It sounded more like a ship pulling up her anchor than the opening of a small front door. But at last he did it, and suddenly he was out in the chilly morning, shivering. He settled himself round the corner with his cheek on the cold concrete, his eye in the wind, and his mind all alert to discover the thief. He had his foot on the next step going up, ready to run when he'd seen what he wanted.

Chapter 10

HE WOULD NEVER have guessed who was doing it. He had the surprise of his life.

He waited and waited in his position till he thought he would set like a model. If he ever moved again it would be all bending over, he thought. Until, first, the milkman came.

Scott watched him carefully. He'd reckoned the milkman as suspect number one.

He watched him leaving nothing at Mr Harding's, one pint at Mrs Prescott's, two pints and a carton of orange at Scott's and a pint at the corner flat.

Everything correct. He was cheerful and whistling – and no wonder why, because Scott could hear the lifts working again.

So that ruled *him* out as the thief.

Next was the paper-girl, a thin kid from the other estate. He knew her from the old days. Scott wouldn't have been a bit surprised to see her put a bottle of milk in her bag. But she came along the balcony and did her job as if she knew she was being watched. She didn't even stop and look at a comic.

And then came a long, long wait. The bottles settled in their wet rings and Scott's legs ached.

It had to be some kid off another balcony, then, Scott thought. Or perhaps whoever had been doing it had stopped. Which meant it would stay looking more like Scott's fault than ever!

It took a lot to make it happen for real, but now, after all he'd tried, Scott started to feel like crying. Taking the blame for something was one thing. But taking the blame and losing your new kitten was a very different matter.

But even as he sniffed and started to swallow, Scott suddenly thought he heard something. What was that? He froze. It wasn't him, definitely. Some sound had come from along the balcony. Someone else was about. The villain, the milk-thief, was moving!

Scott strained his ears, and softly, against the rumble of an early bus and the foggy hoot of a tug, he heard the click of a catch. Followed by a long, careful sigh as a door's edge opened slowly over a mat. His heart seemed to thump loud enough to drown out the sound, and his throat suddenly felt as if it were stuck with a stone. But he'd heard it. He'd heard a door go – and slowly, carefully, he put an eye to the corner and took hold of his breath – while he waited to see which of the flats the thief would come out from.

Chapter 11

IT WAS OLD Mr Harding's. He was in his socks, one trouser-leg rucked and his pyjamas tangled with his braces. The old man crept out into the light and stood and took a long look around – to the left and the right and even over the side. He waited, making sure. Then, as if he'd made up his mind, he took a big breath in, and with a sudden, scary rush of speed, he scurried along the balcony in a bending sort of run. Jerkily, with one bony hand, he scooped at Mrs Prescott's milk. But when his fingers were almost round it, when he was

about to make the grab, all at once he seemed to change his mind. He missed it and went on, with his hand set for Scott's milk instead.

Not so daft! Scott thought. Not so stupid! Taking it in turns with the milk so no one gets too cross! The man who was always ticking him off for doing wrong things!

But that was all Scott had time to think – because he suddenly found himself rushing out from his corner and calling out to Mr Harding.

"Here!" he shouted. "You! Hold on!"

The old man stopped, looked up. He seemed in a daze, all surprised. And for just a second his bent body and the look on his face put Scott in mind of something he'd seen before. In school. In *Help the Old Folk*, when Wayne had tried to run up a drama block with his leg in

a splint. *He'd* been all surprised like that when it had gone wrong.

The picture of him flashed through Scott's mind. And suddenly he found himself talking as if he were in a dream. His voice seemed to have changed its sound, and he didn't know where the words came from.

"Here – daft old milkman's left us extra again, don't want one of our milks, do you?"

Mr Harding was still bending. He was pretending to be sorting out his socks.

"We only wanted one."

"What? Oh, well. Um, ta," he said. he tried to stand up straight. "If it's all right with your mum, then, I'll pay you for it, mind."

"Yeah, 'course. I chased the milkman, but I missed him."

"Oh yes. Lucky for me, eh? I'm chasing him an' all! Forgot to put me note out, didn't I?"

Scott made his laugh sound real. "Well, you won't catch him, not if I can't. He's gone. Lifts are working again today."

"Oh! Oh, well, handy I ran into you, weren't it?"

"S'pose it was."

And with just a nod, Mr Harding went back indoors with a pint of Scott's mother's milk. A bit slower than when he'd come out, but with a slightly straighter back.

Chapter 12

WHAT HAD MADE Scott act like that he
didn't know. It must have been the talk
they'd had at school, he thought. What
had made him act easy on the old bloke
instead of hard must have been the man
from *Help the Old Folk*. Something the
man had said had somehow made him
feel sorry. Like he'd felt sorry for Scrap
in a fix. But Scott didn't go into it too
deeply. He just shrugged his shoulders
and made for his cold front door. He'd
catch it now, making them a pint of
milk short. And he'd still have to work
out a way of letting them know it wasn't

him doing the stealing.

"I heard that."

Scott's heart nearly jumped over the balcony. Pushing quietly at the door to get back in, he'd thought he was on his own.

"I saw it all. I'm not so daft. I've been doing my own watching this morning."

It was Mrs Prescott, ready dressed in her Sunday coat as if it was her turn for a council outing.

"I heard all that – and you done well, Scott. I'm proud of you, you little tyke. You made me pipe me eye." She pulled out a handkerchief from a big, clicky handbag and rolled it round her eyes. "I was dressed ready to frog-march you down to the police," she said. "Instead of which you've made me make a fool of myself. . . ."

Scott stared at her. He really didn't know what to say or do this time.

"Tell you what, you get us a clean piece of paper and I'll put you down for your reward. That's the least I can do."

Scott looked at her, like Scrap had

looked at him. "O.K. Hang on a minute."

"Not in my name, mind. His. Alf Harding's. I'll do a forgery. Make him and me Even-Steven, eh? The crafty old beggar!"

Scott nodded, and smiled.

"Just do me a favour, though. Keep that blessed cat out of my way."

"'Course I will. Scrap won't be no bother."

"And you'd better take this milk back to your school. I've still got the other in the 'fridge."

She handed him that morning's bottle. It was the same milk as the school kitchen had.

"Ta." Getting it back would be dead easy, Scott reckoned.

He pushed at his door. So, he'd done it! He'd made a friend of Mrs Prescott.

And he'd saved Scrap till the council found them a house. Now he suddenly began to feel impatient. Not impatient for his bed. Nor for his breakfast. Not even for a victory stroke of his kitten. But for the funny smell of red dirt and milk which would be waiting for him down at the school. Where he'd get given a clap in the hall, and one of those bouncy super-balls to bring back home for Scrap.

YOUR GUESS IS AS GOOD AS MINE

by Bernard Ashley

Illustrated by David Parkins

The rain hit Nicky hard as he came out of school and everyone ran. It was screams and running feet all along the street, especially when the thunder started. So it seemed too good to be true when he saw his Dad's yellow Mini. But it wasn't his Dad's car, nor was it his Dad driving and Nicky is suddenly plunged into a terrifying adventure and a frantic race against time . . .

0 552 524506

A SELECTED LIST OF TITLES
AVAILABLE FROM YOUNG CORGI BOOKS

THE PRICES SHOWN BELOW WERE CORRECT AT THE TIME OF GOING TO
PRESS. HOWEVER TRANSWORLD PUBLISHERS RESERVE THE RIGHT TO SHOW
NEW RETAIL PRICES ON COVERS WHICH MAY DIFFER FROM THOSE
PREVIOUSLY ADVERTISED IN THE TEXT OR ELSEWHERE.